Dedicated to Gyorgyi and Miklos Gyulassy
(my parents—who have patiently sat through every
sketch and scribble, offering their advice)

Winnie & Waldorf
Copyright © 2015 by Kati Hites
All rights reserved. Manufactured in China.
No part of this book may be used or reproduced in any manner whatsoever without written
permission except in the case of brief quotations embodied in critical articles and reviews. For
information address HarperCollins Children's Books, a division of HarperCollins Publishers,
195 Broadway, New York, NY 10007.
www.harpercollinschildrens.com

ISBN 978-0-06-231161-0

The artist used mixed media to create the digital illustrations for this book.

14 15 16 17 18   SCP   10 9 8 7 6 5 4 3 2 1
❖
First Edition

Winnie & Waldorf

Written and illustrated by Kati Hites

HARPER

An Imprint of HarperCollinsPublishers

This is Waldorf. He is my best friend.
As you can see, he is a great listener.

I always make sure he has
plenty of food and water,

and we pretty much agree on everything.

Usually.

Waldorf is very well behaved,

but sometimes . . . it's up to me to make
sure he doesn't cause any trouble.

My sister Sara's room is
off-limits to everyone,

but Waldorf can't help himself.

I try to get Waldorf to leave, but that's when something terrible happens. . . .

Her special violin!

Just then, Sara walks in. She is not happy.
"WALDORF! Look what you've done!"

"I have a concert tonight!" she yells.
"We should replace you with a cat!"

But Waldorf is part of the family!

It would be the worst thing ever if he got replaced by a cat.

So we decide we must be on our best behavior. We dress up in our most formal attire and are extra polite.

The concert is at our house.
Lots of relatives have come—
even Uncle Stan, who always wears
funny hats.

Waldorf and I notice that Sara looks nervous.

Luckily, my mom was able to fix the violin, but Sara's still not talking to us.

Sara's teacher welcomes everyone and introduces my sister. Sara sits down to play, but nothing happens.

Oh no! Sara is frozen.

Just then, Waldorf sees
the cupcakes!

And Waldorf LOVES cupcakes!

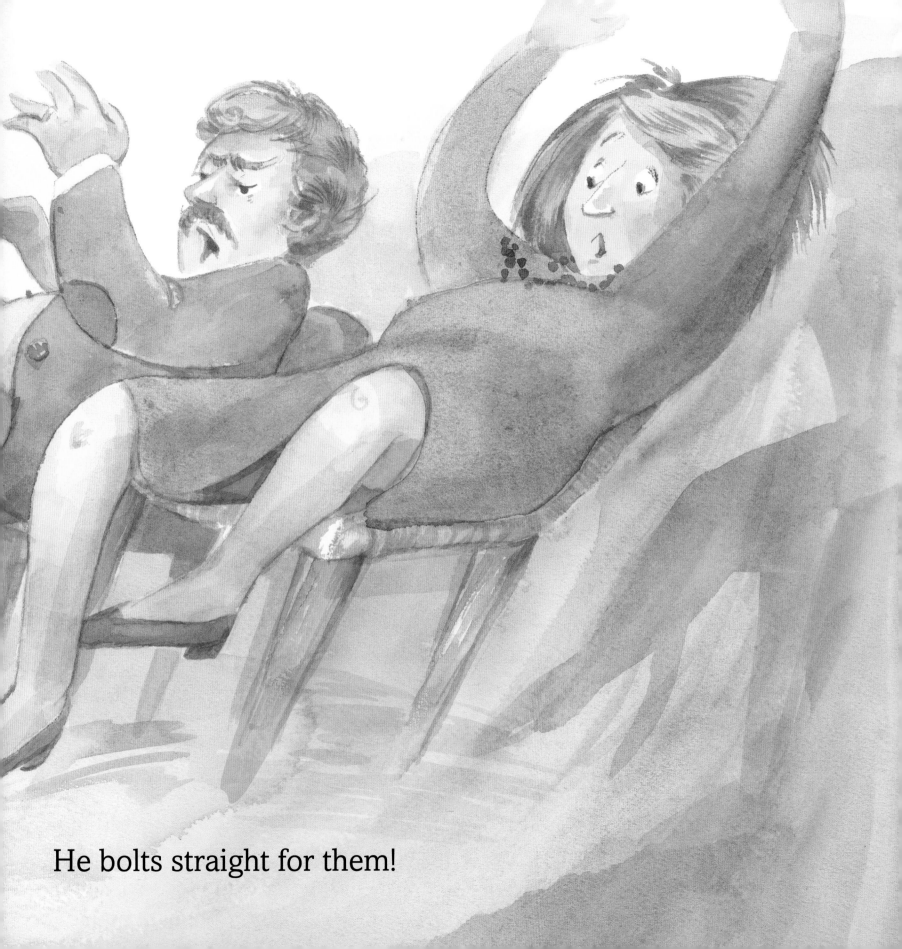

He bolts straight for them!

Waldorf looks ridiculous, which makes everyone laugh . . . including Sara.

Thanks to him, she isn't nervous anymore.

She begins to play, and it sounds beautiful.